'they trai[...]
their vulgar glory
over the fresh
green grass…'

GUY DE MAUPASSANT
Born 1850, Normandy, France
Died 1893, Paris, France

Selection from *A Parisian Affair and Other Stories*,
published in Penguin Classics 2004.

MAUPASSANT IN PENGUIN CLASSICS
A Parisian Affair and Other Stories
Bel-Ami
Pierre et Jean

GUY DE MAUPASSANT

Femme Fatale

Translated by
Siân Miles

PENGUIN BOOKS

PENGUIN CLASSICS

Published by the Penguin Group
Penguin Books Ltd, 80 Strand, London wc2r orl, England
Penguin Group (USA) Inc., 375 Hudson Street, New York, New York 10014, USA
Penguin Group (Canada), 90 Eglinton Avenue East, Suite 700, Toronto,
Ontario, Canada m4p 2y3 (a division of Pearson Penguin Canada Inc.)
Penguin Ireland, 25 St Stephen's Green, Dublin 2, Ireland
(a division of Penguin Books Ltd)
Penguin Group (Australia), 707 Collins Street, Melbourne, Victoria 3008, Australia
(a division of Pearson Australia Group Pty Ltd)
Penguin Books India Pvt Ltd, 11 Community Centre, Panchsheel Park,
New Delhi – 110 017, India
Penguin Group (NZ), 67 Apollo Drive, Rosedale, Auckland 0632, New Zealand
(a division of Pearson New Zealand Ltd)
Penguin Books (South Africa) (Pty) Ltd, Block D, Rosebank Office Park,
181 Jan Smuts Avenue, Parktown North, Gauteng 2193, South Africa

Penguin Books Ltd, Registered Offices: 80 Strand, London wc2r orl, England

www.penguin.com

This selection published in Penguin Classics 2015
001

Translation copyright © Siân Miles, 2004

The moral right of the translator has been asserted

Set in 9/12.4 pt Baskerville 10 Pro
Typeset by Jouve (UK), Milton Keynes
Printed in Great Britain by Clays Ltd, St Ives plc

A CIP catalogue record for this book is available from the British Library

isbn: 978-0-141-39833-4

www.greenpenguin.co.uk

MIX
Paper from
responsible sources
FSC
www.fsc.org FSC™ C018179

Penguin Books is committed to a sustainable
future for our business, our readers and our planet.
This book is made from Forest Stewardship
Council™ certified paper.

Contents

Cockcrow

Madame Berthe d'Avancelles had rejected the advances of her admirer Baron Joseph de Croissard to such an extent that he was now in despair. He had pursued her relentlessly throughout the winter in Paris, and now at his château at Carville in Normandy he was holding a series of hunting parties in her honour.

The husband, Monsieur d'Avancelles, turned a blind eye to all this. It was rumoured that they lived separate lives on account of a physical shortcoming of his which Madame could not overlook. He was a fat little man with short arms, short legs, a short neck, short nose, short everything in fact.

Madame d'Avancelles, in contrast, was a tall, chestnut-haired, determined-looking young woman. She laughed openly at old Pipe and Slippers as she called him to his face but looked with tender indulgence on her admirer, the titled Baron Joseph de Croissard, with his broad shoulders, his sturdy neck and his fair, drooping moustache.

Until now, however, she had granted him no favours despite the fact that he was spending a fortune on her, throwing a constant round of receptions, hunting parties, and all kinds of celebrations to which he invited the local aristocracy.

All day long the woods rang to the sound of hounds in full cry after a fox or a wild boar and every night a dazzling display of fireworks spiralled upwards to join the sparkling stars. A tracery of light from the drawing-room windows shone on the huge lawns where shadowy figures occasionally passed.

It was the russet season of autumn when leaves swirled over the gardens like flocks of birds. Wafting on the air came the tang of damp, bare earth, caught as the smell of a woman's naked flesh as her gown slips down to the floor after the ball.

On an evening during a reception held the previous spring, Madame d'Avancelles had replied to an imploring Monsieur de Croissard with the words: 'If I am to fall at all, my friend, it will certainly not be before the leaves do likewise. I've far too many things to do this summer to give it a thought.' He had remembered those daring words of hers spoken so provocatively and was now pressing his advantage. Each day he crept closer, gaining more and more of the bold beauty's heart until by this point her resistance seemed hardly more than symbolic.

Soon there was to be a great hunting party. The night before, Madame Berthe had said laughingly to the Baron: 'Tomorrow, Baron, if you manage to kill the beast I shall have something to give you.'

He was up at dawn reconnoitring where the wild boar was wallowing. He accompanied his whips, setting out the order of the hunt in such a way that he should return from the field in triumph. When the horns sounded for the meet, he appeared in a well-cut hunting costume of scarlet and gold. With his upright, broad-chested figure and flashing eyes he glowed with good health and manly vigour.

The hunt moved off. The boar was raised and ran, followed

by the baying hounds rushing through the undergrowth. The horses broke into a gallop, hurtling with their riders along the narrow forest paths while far behind the following carriages drove noiselessly over the softer verges.

Teasingly, Madame d'Avancelles kept the Baron at her side, slowing down to walking pace in an interminably long, straight avenue along which four rows of oaks arched vault-like towards each other. Trembling with both desire and frustration he listened with one ear to the young woman's light badinage, the other pricked for the hunting horns and the sound of the hounds growing fainter by the minute.

'So you love me no longer,' she was saying.

'How can you say such a thing?' he replied.

'You do seem to be more interested in the hunt than in me,' she went on. He groaned. 'You do remember your own orders don't you? To kill the beast myself.'

'Indeed I do,' she added with great seriousness. 'Before my very eyes.' At this he quivered impatiently in the saddle, spurred on his eager horse and finally lost his patience.

'For God's sake, Madame, not if we stay here a minute longer.'

'That is how it has to be nevertheless,' she cried laughingly. 'Otherwise, you're out of luck.'

Then she spoke to him gently, leaning her hand on his arm and, as if absentmindedly, stroking his horse's mane. They had turned right on to a narrow path overhung with trees when, suddenly swerving to avoid one of their low branches, she leaned against him so closely that he felt her hair tickling his neck. He threw his arms around her and pressing his thick moustache to her forehead planted upon it a passionate kiss.

At first she was motionless, stunned by his ardour, then with a start she turned her head and, either by chance or design, her own delicate lips met his beneath their blond cascade. Then, out of either embarrassment or regret for the incident she spurred her horse on the flank and galloped swiftly away. For a long while they rode straight on together, without so much as exchanging a glance.

The hunt in full cry was close and the thickets seemed to shake, when suddenly, covered in blood and shaking off the hounds that clung to him, the boar went rushing past through the bushes. The Baron gave a triumphant laugh, cried 'Let him who loves me follow me!' and disappeared, swallowed up by the forest. When Madame d'Avancelles reached an open glade a few minutes later he was just getting up, covered with mud, his jacket torn and his hands bloody, while the animal lay full length on the ground with the Baron's knife plunged up to the hilt in its shoulder.

The quarry was cut by torchlight on that mild and melancholy night. The moon gilded the red flames of the torches which filled the air with pine smoke. The dogs, yelping and snapping, devoured the stinking innards of the boar while the beaters and the gentlemen, standing in a circle around the spoil, blew their horns with all their might. The flourish of the hunting horns rose into the night air above the woods. Its echoes fell and were lost in the distant valleys beyond, alarming nervous stags, a barking fox and small grey rabbits at play on the edge of the glades. Terrified night birds fluttered above the crazed pack while the women, excited a little by the violence and vulnerability surrounding these events,

leaned a little heavily on the men's arms and, without waiting
for the hounds to finish, drifted off with their partners down
the many forest paths. Feeling languid after all the exhaust-
ing emotion of the day Madame d'Avancelles said to the
Baron: 'Would you care for a turn in the park, my friend?'

He gave no answer, but trembling and unsteady with
desire pulled her to him. Instantly they kissed and as they
walked very slowly under the almost leafless trees through
which moonlight filtered, their love, their desire and their
need for each other was so intense that they almost sank
down at the foot of a tree.

The horns had fallen silent and the exhausted hounds were
sleeping by now in their kennels.

'Let us go back,' the young woman said. They returned.

Just as they reached the château and were about to enter,
she murmured in a faint voice: 'I'm so tired, my friend, I'm
going straight to bed.' As he opened his arms for one last
kiss she fled, with the parting words: 'No ... to sleep ...
but ... let him who loves me follow me!'

An hour later when the whole sleeping château seemed
dead to the world the Baron crept on tiptoe out of his room
and scratched at the door of his friend. Receiving no reply
he made to open it and found it unbolted.

She was leaning dreamily with her elbows on the window
ledge. He threw himself at her knees which he showered with
mad kisses through her nightdress. She said nothing, but
ran her dainty fingers caressingly through the Baron's hair.
Suddenly, as if coming to a momentous decision, she disen-
gaged herself and whispered provocatively: 'Wait for me. I

shall be back.' Her finger raised in shadow pointed to the far end of the room where loomed the vague white shape of her bed.

With wildly trembling hands he undressed quickly by feel and slipped between the cool sheets. He stretched out in bliss and almost forgot his friend as his weary body yielded to the linen's caress. Doubtless enjoying the strain on his patience, still she did not return. He closed his eyes in exquisitely pleasurable anticipation. His most cherished dream was about to come true. Little by little his limbs relaxed, as did his mind, where thoughts drifted, vague and indistinct. He succumbed at last to the power of great fatigue and finally fell asleep.

He slept the heavy, impenetrable sleep of the exhausted huntsman. He slept indeed till dawn. Then from a nearby tree through the still half-open window came the ringing cry of a cock. Startled awake, the Baron's eyes flew open. Finding himself, to his great surprise, in a strange bed and with a woman's body lying against his he remembered nothing and stammered as he struggled into consciousness: 'What? Where am I? What is it?'

At this, she, who had not slept a wink, looked at the puffy, red-eyed and dishevelled man at her side. She answered in the same dismissive tone she took with her husband. 'Nothing,' she said, 'it's a cock. Go back to sleep, Monsieur. It's nothing to do with you.'

Femme Fatale

The restaurant, Le Grillon, Mecca of the entire local boating community, was now slowly emptying. At the main entrance a large crowd of people were calling and shouting out to each other. With oars on their shoulders, strapping great fellows in white jerseys waved and gesticulated. Women in light spring frocks were stepping cautiously into the skiffs moored alongside and, having settled themselves in the stern of each, were smoothing out their dresses. The owner of the establishment, a tough-looking, red-bearded man of legendary strength, was helping the pretty young things aboard and with a practised hand was holding steady the gently bobbing craft.

The oarsmen then took their places, playing to the gallery and showing off broad chests and muscular arms in their sleeveless vests. The gallery in this case consisted of a crowd of suburbanites in their Sunday best, as well as a few workmen and some soldiers, all leaning on the parapet of the bridge and watching the scene below with keen interest. One by one the boats cast off from the landing stage. The oarsmen leaned forward and with a regular swing pulled back. At each stroke of the long, slightly curved blades the fast skiffs sped through the water making for La Grenouillère and growing progressively smaller till they disappeared beyond the railway bridge and into the distance.

Only one couple now remained. The slim, pale-faced young man, still a relatively beardless youth, had his arm around the waist of his girl, a skinny little grasshopper of a creature with brown hair. They stopped from time to time to gaze into each other's eyes.

The owner cried: 'Come on, Monsieur Paul, get a move on!'

The couple moved down closer. Of all the customers, Monsieur Paul, who paid regularly and in full, was the best liked and most respected. Many of the others ran up bills and frequently absconded without settling them. The son of a senator, he was also an excellent advertisement for the establishment. When some stranger asked, 'And who's that young chap over there with his eyes glued to the girl?' one of the regulars would murmur, in a mysterious, important sort of way, 'Oh, that's Paul Baron, you know, the son of the senator.' Then the stranger would inevitably have to comment, 'Poor young devil, he's got it bad.' The proprietress of Le Grillon, a good businesswoman and wise in the ways of the world, called the young man and his companion 'my two turtle doves' and looked with tender indulgence on the love affair which brought such glamour to her establishment.

The couple ambled slowly down to where a skiff called the *Madeleine* was ready. Before embarking, however, they stopped to kiss once more, much to the amusement of the audience gathered on the bridge. Finally, Monsieur Paul took up the oars and set off after the others also making for La Grenouillère.

When they arrived it was getting on for three and here too the vast floating café was swarming with people. It is in effect one huge raft with a tarpaulin roof supported by wooden columns. It is connected to the charming island of Croissy by two narrow footbridges, one of which runs right through to the centre of the café itself. The other connects at the far end with a tiny islet where a single tree grows and which is nicknamed the Pot-de-Fleurs. From there it connects with the land again via a bathing pool.

Monsieur Paul moored his boat alongside the café, climbed up to its balustrade then, holding his girl's two hands, guided her up also. They entered, found a place for two at the end of a table and sat down opposite each other.

Lining the towpath on the opposite side of the river was a long string of vehicles. Fiacres alternated with the flashy carriages of gay young men-about-town. The first were lumbering great hulks whose bodywork crushed the springs beneath and to which were harnessed broken-down old hacks with drooping necks. The other carriages were streamlined, with light suspension and fine, delicate wheels. These were drawn by horses with slender, straight, strong legs, heads held high and bits snowy with foam. Their solemn, liveried drivers, heads held stiffly inside huge collars, sat ramrod straight with their whips resting on their knees.

The river banks were crowded with people coming and going in different kinds of configurations: family parties, groups of friends, couples and individuals. They idly plucked at blades of grass, wandered down to the water's edge then climbed back up to the path. Having reached a certain spot they all congregated to wait for the ferryman whose heavy boat plied constantly back and forth, depositing passengers on the island.

The branch of the river, incidentally called the dead

branch, which this floating bar dominates, seemed asleep, so slowly did the current move there. Flotillas of gigs, skiffs, canoes, pedaloes and river craft of all kinds streamed over the still water, mingling and intersecting, meeting and parting, running foul of each other, stopping, and with a sudden jerk of their oarsmen's arms and a tensing of their muscles, taking off again, darting this way and that like shoals of red and yellow fish.

More were arriving all the time; some from Chatou upstream, some from Bougival, downstream. Gales of contagious laughter carried from one boat to another and the air was full of insults, complaints, protestations and howls. The men in the boats exposed their muscular, tanned bodies to the glare of the sun and, like exotic water-plants, the women's parasols of red, green and yellow silk blossomed in the sterns of their craft.

The July sun blazed in the middle of the sky and the atmosphere was gay and carefree, while in the windless air not a leaf stirred in the poplars and willows lining the banks of the river. In the distance ahead, the conspicuous bulk of Mont-Valérien loomed, rearing the ramparts of its fortifications in the glare of the sun. On the right, the gentle slopes of Louveciennes, following the curve of the river, formed a semi-circle within which could be glimpsed, through the dense and shady greenery of their spacious lawns, the white-painted walls of weekend retreats.

On the land adjoining La Grenouillère strollers were sauntering under the gigantic trees which help to make this part of the island one of the most delightful parks imaginable. Busty women with peroxided hair and nipped-in waists could be seen, made up to the nines with blood red lips and black-kohled eyes. Tightly laced into their garish dresses they trailed in all their vulgar glory over the fresh green grass. They were accompanied by men whose fashion-plate accessories, light gloves, patent-leather boots, canes as slender as threads and absurd monocles made them look like complete idiots.

The part of the island facing La Grenouillère is narrow and between it and the opposite bank where another ferry plies, bringing people over from Croissy, the current is very strong and very fast. Here it swirls and roars, raging like a torrent in a myriad of eddies and foam. A detachment of pontoon-builders wearing the uniform of artillerymen was camped on the bank and some of the soldiers, side by side on a long beam of wood, sat watching the river below.

A noisy, rambunctious crowd filled the floating restaurant. The wooden tables, sticky and awash with streams of spilt drink, were covered with half-empty glasses and surrounded by half-tipsy customers. The crowd sang and shouted and brawled. Red-faced, belligerent men, their hats tipped at the backs of their heads and their eyes glassy with booze, prowled like animals spoiling for a fight. The women, cadging free drinks in the meantime, were seeking their prey for the night. The space between the tables was filled with the usual clientèle – noisy young boating blades and their female companions in short flannel skirts.

One of the men was banging away at the piano using his feet as well as his hands. Four couples were dancing a quadrille and watching them was a group of elegantly dressed young men whose respectable appearance was ruined by the hideous incongruity of the setting.

The place reeked of vice and corruption and the dregs of Parisian society in all its rottenness gathered there: cheats, conmen and cheap hacks rubbed shoulders with under-age dandies, old roués and rogues, sleazy underworld types once notorious for things best forgotten mingled with other small-time crooks and speculators, dabblers in dubious ventures, frauds, pimps, and racketeers. Cheap sex, both male and female, was on offer in this tawdry meat-market of a place where petty rivalries were exploited, and quarrels picked over nothing in an atmosphere of fake gallantry where swords or pistols at dawn settled matters of highly questionable honour in the first place.

Every Sunday, out of sheer curiosity some of the people from the surrounding countryside would drop in. Every year would bring a fresh batch of young men, extremely young men at that, keen to make useful contacts. Casual cruisers would amble by and every so often a complete innocent would become embroiled.

La Grenouillère lived up to its name. There was a place for bathing between the tarpaulin-covered raft where drinks were served and the Pot-de-Fleurs. Women with the requisite curves came there to display their wares and their clients. Those less fortunate who required padding and corsetry to pass muster looked disdainfully on as their rivals cavorted and splashed about.

Awaiting their turn to plunge in and thronging around a small diving board were swimmers of every shape and size: some slim and straight as vine-poles, some round as pumpkins, some gnarled as olive-branches, some with bodies curved forward over pot-bellies, some whose vast stomachs threw the body backwards. Each was as ugly as the other as they leapt into the water and splashed the customers drinking at the café next door.

Despite the proximity of the river and the huge trees shading it, the place was suffocatingly hot. Mingling with the fumes of spilt drinks came the smell of flesh and the cheap perfume with which the skin of those trading in sex was drenched. Underlying all these smells was the slight but persistent aroma of talc, which wafted with varying intensity as if an unseen hand were waving some gigantic powder-puff over the entire scene.

All eyes were on the river where the comings and goings of the boats attracted everyone's attention. Girls sprawled in the stern opposite their strong-wristed menfolk looked with contempt at those still prowling about the island in search of a male to buy them dinner that night. Sometimes when a crew in full swing flashed past their friends ashore would shout and were joined by the crazy, yelling crowd inside the restaurant. At the bend of the river near Chatou boats were constantly coming into view. As they approached and grew more distinct, faces became recognizable and more shouts went up.

A boat with an awning and containing four women came slowly downstream towards them. The woman at the oars was small, lean and past her prime. She wore her hair pinned up inside an oilskin hat. Opposite her a big blonde dressed in a man's jacket was lying on her back at the bottom of the boat with a foot resting on the thwart on either side of the oarswoman. The blonde was smoking a cigarette and with each jerk of the oars her bosom and her belly quivered. At the very stern of the boat under the awning two beautiful, tall, slender girls, one blonde the other brunette, sat with their arms round each other's waists watching their two companions.

A shout went up from La Grenouillère: 'Aye-aye! Lesbos!' and suddenly a wild clamour broke out. In the terrifying scramble to see, glasses were knocked over and people started climbing on the tables. Everyone began to chant 'Lesbos! Lesbos! Lesbos!' The words merged into a vague howl before suddenly starting up again, rising into the air, filling the plain beyond, resounding in the dense foliage of the tall surrounding trees and echoing in the distance as if aimed at the sun itself.

During this ovation the oarswoman had calmly come to a halt. The big blonde lying at the bottom of the boat turned her head languorously and raised herself on her elbows. The two in the stern started laughing and waving to the crowd. At this there was even more of a hullabaloo and the place shook with the noise. The men raised their hats and the women waved their handkerchiefs. Every voice, deep and shrill alike, chanted in unison 'Lesbos!' This motley collection of undesirables seemed to be saluting a leader, as warships give a gun salute to their passing admiral. From the flotilla of boats also there was wild acclamation for the women's boat which now continued at its leisurely pace, to land a little further off.

Monsieur Paul's reaction was unlike that of the others. Pulling a key from his pocket he started using it as a whistle and blew hard. His girl, looking nervous now and even paler than before, pulled his arm to make him stop. This time when she looked into his eyes, it was with fury. But he was beside himself with male jealousy and a deep, instinctive ungovernable rage. His lips trembling with indignation he stammered: 'Shouldn't be allowed! They should be drowned like puppies with stones round their necks!'

Madeleine suddenly lost her temper. Her shrill voice became piercing as she lashed out at him: 'Mind your own business, will you! They've got a perfect right to do whatever they want. They're not doing any harm to anyone. Why don't you just shut up and leave them alone . . .'

He cut her short. 'This a matter for the police! If it was up to me I'd have them locked up in Saint-Lazare!'

She gave a start. 'Oh you would, would you?'

'Certainly I would. And in the meantime I forbid you to have anything to do with them. I absolutely forbid it, do you understand?'

She shrugged her shoulders at this and said in a suddenly calm voice: 'Listen, dear, I shall do exactly as I please. If you don't like it you know what you can do. Get the hell out. Now. I'm not your wife, so shut up.'

He remained silent and they stood staring each other out, breathing rapidly, their mouths set.

At the other end of the café the women were now making their entrance. The two dressed as men led, one gaunt and weatherbeaten, ageing and very mannish. The other, more than amply filling the white flannel outfit with her large bottom and her huge thighs encased in the wide trousers, waddled forward like a fat, bow-legged goose. The two friends followed and the whole boating community surged forward to shake hands.

The four had rented a riverside cottage and lived together

there as two couples. Their vice was public, official and perfectly obvious to all. It was referred to quite naturally as
something entirely normal. There were rumours about jeal-
ous scenes that took place there and about the various
actresses and other famous women who frequented the little
cottage near the water's edge. One neighbour, scandalized
by the goings-on, alerted the police at one stage and an
inspector accompanied by one of his men came to make
enquiries. It was a delicate mission: there was nothing the
women could be prosecuted for, least of all prostitution. The
inspector was deeply puzzled and could not understand
what these alleged misdemeanours could possibly be. He
asked a whole lot of pointless questions, compiled a lengthy
report and dismissed the charges out of hand. The joke
spread as far as Saint-Germain.

Like queens they now walked slowly the entire length of
La Grenouillère. They seemed happy to be in the limelight
and delighted with the attention paid to them by all this
riff-raff. Madeleine and her lover watched them, and as they
approached the girl's face lit up.

When the leading couple reached their table Madeleine
cried 'Pauline!' and the big girl, turning round, stopped,
still arm in arm with her midshipwoman.

'Well good heavens! Madeleine! Darling! Come and join
us for a bit. We must catch up!'

Paul tightened his grip on his girl's wrist but she said, 'You
know what you can do, sweetheart, shove off.'

He kept quiet and let her be. Standing huddled together
the women continued their animated conversation *sotto voce*.
Pauline from time to time cast furtive glances at Paul and

flashed him an evil, sardonic smile. Finally, unable to bear it a minute longer he suddenly stood up and trembling in every limb leapt towards her. He seized Madeleine by the shoulders and said: 'Come with me, do you hear? I said you were not to speak to these beastly women!'

Raising her voice, Pauline began to swear at him like a fishwife. People around started laughing. Others stood on tip-toe to get a better look. Under the hail of filthy abuse he was speechless. Feeling contaminated by it and fearing there might be worse to come he retreated, retraced his steps and went to lean on the balustrade overlooking the river, turning his back on the three triumphant women. He stayed there looking at the water and every so often brusquely wiping away the tears that sprang to his eyes.

The fact was that despite himself, without knowing why or how it had happened and very much against his better judgement, he had fallen hopelessly in love. He had fallen as if into some deep and muddy hole. By nature he was a delicate and sensitive soul. He had had ideals and dreamed of an exquisite and passionate affair. And now he had fallen for this little cricket of a creature. She was as stupid as every other woman and not even pretty to make up for it. Skinny and foul-tempered, she had taken possession of him entirely from tip to toe, body and soul. He had fallen under the omnipotent and mysterious spell of the female. He was overwhelmed by this colossal force of unknown origin, the demon in the flesh capable of hurling the most rational man in the world at the feet of a worthless harlot. There was no way he could explain its fatal and total power.

Behind his back now he could feel something evil brewing.

Their laughter pierced his heart. What should he do? He knew very well but had not the courage. He stared fixedly at the opposite bank where an angler was fishing, his line perfectly still. All of a sudden the man jerked out of the water a little silver fish which wriggled at the end of his line. Twisting and turning it this way and that he tried to extract his hook, but in vain. Losing patience he started pulling and, as he did so, tore out the entire bloody gullet of the fish with parts of its intestines attached. Paul shuddered, feeling himself equally torn apart. It seemed to him that the hook was like his own love and that if he were to tear it out he too would be gutted by a piece of curved wire hooked deep into his essential self at the end of a line held by Madeleine.

Feeling a hand on his shoulder he started and turned round. Madeleine was standing beside him. Neither spoke. She simply put her elbows on the balustrade beside him and leaned with him, staring out at the river. He tried to think of something to say but failed. He was incapable of analysing what was going on inside him. All he felt now was joy in the very nearness of her and a shameful cowardice on his own part. He wanted to forgive her, to let her do anything in the world she liked provided she never left him again.

After a while in a very gentle voice he asked, 'Would you like to leave now? We'll be better off in the boat.'

'All right my pet,' she said.

Awash with forgiveness and with tears still in his eyes he held her two hands tightly and helped her on board. Basking in the warmth of the afternoon they rowed upstream again past the willows and the grass-covered banks. When they reached Le Grillon once more it was not yet six, so, leaving their skiff, they set off on foot towards Bezons across the meadows and past the high poplars bordering the banks.

The wide hayfields waiting to be harvested were full of flowers. The sinking sun cast a mantle of russet light over all and in the gentle warmth of the day's end the fragrance of the grass wafted in on them mingling with the damp smells of the river and filling the air with easy languor and an atmosphere of blessed well-being.

He felt soft and unresistant, in communion with the calm splendour of the evening and with the vague, mysterious thrill of life itself. He felt in tune with the all-embracing poetry of the moment in which plants and all that surrounded him revealed themselves to his senses at this lovely restful and reflective time of day. He was sensitive to it all but she appeared totally unaffected. They were walking side by side when suddenly, bored by the silence, she began to sing. In a squeaky, unmodulated voice she sang one of the catchy tunes of the day which jarred violently with the deeply serene mood of the evening. He looked at her and felt between them an unbridgeable abyss. She was swinging her parasol through the grass with her head down, looking at her feet as she sang, drawing out the notes and adding the odd little trill.

So behind the smooth little brow which he so much adored there was nothing! Absolutely nothing! Its sole concern at the moment was this caterwauling. The thoughts which from time to time passed through it were as vapid as the music. She had no understanding of him. They were as separate and distinct as if they had never met. His kisses had touched her lips only and nothing deeper within.

When, however, she raised her eyes to meet his and smiled,

he felt himself melt. Opening his arms out wide to her in a surge of renewed love he clasped her passionately to him. Since he was crushing her dress as he did so, she eventually broke free saying consolingly, 'Yes, yes, I love you, my pet, now that's enough.' In a mad rush of relief he grabbed her round the waist and started to run, dragging her with him. He kissed her on the cheeks, the temples and the neck, all the time dancing with joy. They threw themselves down at the edge of a thicket incandescent in the light of the setting sun. Even before catching their breath they came together. She could not understand the rapture he felt.

Walking back hand in hand they suddenly saw through the trees the river and on it the boat containing the four women. Big Pauline must have caught sight of them at the same time since she straightened up, blew kisses at Madeleine and shouted, 'See you tonight!'

'See you tonight!' shouted Madeleine in reply.

Paul felt his heart turn suddenly to ice. They returned for dinner and settling down in one of the arbours at the side of the water they began to eat in silence. When darkness fell, a candle enclosed in a globe was brought which shed a feeble, glimmering light on the two. All the time they could hear bursts of laughter coming from the large room on the first floor where the boat-trippers were. The couple were just about to order dessert when Paul, taking Madeleine's hand tenderly in his own, said: 'Darling, I feel so tired. Shall we make an early night of it?'

But she saw through his little ploy and shot him an enigmatic glance, one of those treacherous looks that so often appear in women's eyes. She thought for a second, then said, 'You're perfectly welcome to go to bed if you like but I've promised to go to the dance at La Grenouillère.'

Attempting to mask his misery he gave her a pitiful smile and answered in a coaxing, wheedling tone: 'Be a darling. Let's both stay here. Please.'

She shook her head without saying a word. He tried again. 'Please, sweetheart . . .'

She cut him off. 'You know what I said. If you're not happy, you know where the door is. Nobody's stopping you. But I've promised, and I'm going.'

He put his two elbows on the table, sank his head into his hands and sat brooding. The trippers were coming down the stairs, yelling as usual before setting off for the dance at La Grenouillère. Madeleine said to Paul: 'Make up your mind. If you're not coming I'll ask one of these gentlemen to take me there.'

Paul rose. 'Come on then,' he muttered before they too set off. The night was dark and the sky full of stars. Around them the air was still hot and the atmosphere heavy with seething, unseen activity. The warm breeze caressed their faces, its hot breath stifling their own and making them gasp slightly. The skiffs set off, each with a Venetian lantern in the prow. It was too dark to see anything of the boats themselves except for the little patches of colour in the night bobbing and dancing like frenzied glow-worms. Voices sounded from the shadows on all sides as the young couple's skiff glided gently along. Sometimes when another overtook they would catch the flash of the oarsman's white-jerseyed back illuminated by his lantern. As they came round the bend of the river, La Grenouillère came into sight in the distance.

In gala mood, the place was decorated with bunting and with strings, clusters and garlands of fairy lights. On the surface of the Seine large barges moved slowly about, representing domes, pyramids and all kinds of monuments picked out in variously coloured lights. Illuminated festoons hung down as far as the water itself, and here and there an enormous red or blue lantern suspended from an invisible rod hung like a huge star in the sky.

All these illuminations shone on the café and floodlit the great trees on the bank whose trunks stood out pale grey and whose leaves were milky green against the deep, pitch black of the fields and of the sky. A band consisting of five local players blared shrill, syncopated music across the water and, hearing it, Madeleine began to sing along. She wanted to go in right away. Paul would have preferred to make a tour of the island first but had to give in. The clientèle had thinned out a little by this time, still consisting mostly of boatmen with the odd sprinkling of middle-class couples and a few young men flanked by girls. The director and organizer of the can-can strutted in his faded black suit and cast round the audience the world-weary, professional eye of a cheap music-hall master of ceremonies. Paul was relieved to see that Big Pauline and her chums were nowhere to be seen.

People were dancing. Couples faced each other and capered about madly, kicking their legs as high as their partners' noses. The women, who appeared to have double-jointed legs and hips, leapt about in a frou-frou of lifted skirts, flashing their knickers and kicking their legs up over their heads with amazing agility. They wriggled their bellies and shook their bosoms, spreading about them the powerful smell of female flesh in sweat. The males squatted like toads in front of them making faces and obscene gestures. They cavorted and turned cartwheels, posturing meanwhile in hideous parody, as one strapping maid and two waiters served the audience drinks.

Since the café-boat was covered by a roof only and had no side walls to separate it from the outdoors, the whole rumbustious dance was performed against the backdrop of the peaceful night and a firmament dusted with stars. Suddenly Mont-Valérien in the distance lit up as if a fire had started behind it. The glow deepened and spread, describing a wide, luminous circle of pale light. Then a ruby-coloured shape appeared, grew large, and glowed like red-hot metal. The circle widened further still and seemed to be emerging from the earth itself, as the moon, breaking free of the horizon, sailed gently upwards into space. As it rose, its crimson glow dimmed and turned to an increasingly light then bright yellow. As the planet climbed higher it grew smaller and smaller still in the distance.

Paul, lost in long contemplation of this sight, had become oblivious of his girl. When he turned round she had disappeared from view. He looked for her in vain. Having searched anxiously and systematically up and down the rows of tables he started asking people. No one had seen her. He then began to wander about wretchedly until one of the waiters said: 'If you're looking for Madame Madeleine, she went off a little while ago with Madame Pauline.'

Simultaneously, he caught sight of the midshipwoman and

the two beautiful girls sitting at the opposite end of the café, arms round each other's waists, watching him and whispering. Realizing what had happened, he ran off like a madman towards the island. Chasing first in the direction of Chatou, he stopped at the edge of the plain, turned and retraced his steps. He began to search the dense coppices, wandering about aimlessly and stopping every so often to listen. All he could hear around him was the short, metallic croak of frogs. Towards Bougival an unfamiliar bird sang a song which reached him faintly from a distance. Over the broad fields the moon shed a soft, filmy light. It filtered through the foliage, silvering the barks of the poplars and casting a shower of brilliant moonbeams on the shimmering tops of the tallest trees. Despite himself Paul was enchanted by the intoxicating loveliness of the night. It penetrated the terrible anguish he was feeling and stirred in his heart a fierce sense of irony. He longed with all his gentle and idealistic soul for a faithful woman to worship – someone in whose arms he could express all his love and tenderness as well as his passion.

Choked by racking sobs, he had to stop in his tracks. Having recovered a little he went on, only to feel a sudden stab in his heart. There, behind that bush . . . a pair of lovers! He ran forward and saw their silhouettes united in a seemingly endless kiss before they quickly ran off at his approach. He dared not call out, knowing full well that his own girl would not respond. He was desperately afraid now of coming upon them all of a sudden. The music of the quadrilles with its piercing solo cornets, the mock gaiety of the flute and the scraping of the fiddles pulled at his own heartstrings and deepened the pain he continued to feel.

Suddenly it occurred to him that she might have gone back in! Yes, that was it! She must have returned. He had lost all sense of proportion, he was stupid, he had been carried away by all the silly suspicions and fears that always haunted him. In one of those periods of strange calm which occur during periods of the blackest despair he turned and began to make for the café again.

He took in the whole room at a single glance. She was not there. He checked all the tables, and once again came face to face with the three women. He must have looked the picture of dejection for the three burst out laughing. Rushing out again, he ran back to the island. He threw himself into the coppices and stopped to listen once more. It was some time before he could hear anything save the roaring in his own ears. Finally, however, he thought he could hear some way ahead a shrill little laugh he knew only too well. Creeping forward he fell to his knees and crawled on, parting the branches cautiously as he went. His heart was beating so wildly in his chest that he could hardly breathe. Two voices were murmuring. He could not make out what they were saying. Then they fell silent again.

He had a sudden furious desire to run away, not to see, not to know and to keep on running to escape from the raging passion with which he was consumed. He would return to Chatou, catch a train and never come back. He would never see her again. Just as suddenly her face appeared in his mind's eye. He saw her as she was waking up next to him in their warm bed. He saw her snuggle up to him and throw her arms round his neck. Her hair was loose and a little tangled over her brow. Her eyes were still closed and her lips parted, waiting for the first kiss of the day. The thought of this morning's embrace filled him with unbearable regret and frantic desire.

They were talking again. He approached bent double. Then a cry rose from under the branches close to him. That cry! It was one of those he had come to know from their most tender, their most passionate love-making. He crept even closer, drawn irresistibly, blindly, despite himself . . . and then he saw them.

Oh! If only the other person had been a man! But this! He was transfixed by the loathsome sight before him. He remained there overwhelmed by shock. It was as though he had just stumbled upon the mutilated body of a loved one. It was a crime against nature, a monstrous and wicked desecration. Suddenly flashing into his mind's eye this time came the image of the little fish whose entrails he had earlier seen ripped out. Madeleine was moaning 'Pauline', exactly as she used to moan 'Paul' to him. Hearing it, he felt such pain that he turned and fled. He hurtled into one tree and ricocheted into another, fell over a root, picked himself up and ran again until suddenly he found himself at the edge of the river. The raging torrent made whirls and eddies on which the moonbeams now played. On the opposite side the bank loomed over the water like a cliff, leaving a wide band of black at its foot from which the sound of the swirling water rose in the darkness. Clearly visible on the other side were the weekend homes at Croissy.

Paul saw all this as if in a dream or as something remembered. He was no longer thinking. He understood nothing now. Everything including his own existence seemed vague, distant, forgotten and finished. There was the river. Did he know what he was doing? Did he want to die? He had lost his mind. Nevertheless he turned round to face the island where she was. Into the night in which the faint but persistent beat of the dance-band still throbbed back and forth, he shouted, 'Madeleine!'

His heart-rending call pierced the great silence of the sky and echoed, lost in the distance. Then with a furious animal-like leap he plunged into the river. The water splashed then closed over the spot setting up a series of ever-widening circles which rippled in the moonlight as far as the opposite bank. The two women had heard. Madeleine got up and said, 'That's Paul.' A suspicion arose suddenly in her mind. 'He's drowned himself,' she said and rushed towards the bank where Pauline caught up with her.

A heavy punt with two men in it was circling over and over around the same spot. One of the men rowed while the other was plunging a long pole into the water evidently looking for something. Pauline shouted: 'What's happened? What are you doing?'

A stranger's voice cried: 'A man's just drowned himself.'

With haggard faces the two women huddled together and watched the boat's manoeuvres. The music from La Grenouillère pounding in the distance provided a grim counterpoint to the movements of the solemn fishermen. The river, now containing a corpse in its depths, continued to swirl in the moonlight. The search was prolonged and

27

Madeleine, waiting in horrible suspense, shivered. Finally, after a good half-hour, one of the men announced: 'I've got him!'

Very gradually he pulled in the boathook. A large mass appeared at the surface of the water. The other boatman left his oars and between the two, each heaving with all his strength, they managed to haul the inert body and bring it tumbling into the boat. They soon reached the bank and found an open, flat space in the moonlight. As they landed, the women approached.

As soon as she saw him Madeleine recoiled in horror. In the light of the moon's rays he looked green already and his mouth, his eyes, his nose and his clothes were full of the river's slime. The stiff fingers of his clenched fist looked hideous. Black, liquid silt covered his entire body. The face looked swollen and from his hair now plastered down with ooze a stream of filthy water ran. The two men examined him.

'You know him?' asked one.

The other, the Croissy ferryman, hesitated.

'Seems to me I know the face . . .,' he said, 'but it's difficult to tell seeing him like this . . .'

Then suddenly: 'Oh! I know! It's Monsieur Paul!'

'Who's Monsieur Paul?' his friend asked.

The first went on: 'You know! Monsieur Paul Baron. Son of that senator. The kid who was so hooked on that girl, you remember?'

The other added philosophically: 'No more girls for him now, eh? Poor sod. And with all that money too!'

Madeleine, having collapsed on the ground, was sobbing.

Pauline approached the body and said, 'I suppose he really is dead . . . there's no chance he might . . . ?'

The men shrugged their shoulders.

'After that length of time no question.'

Then one of them asked: 'Was he staying at Le Grillon?'

'Yes,' said the other. 'We'd better take him back there. Handsome tip, mate.' Re-embarking they set off, moving slowly against the rapid current. Long after they had disappeared from the two women's sight the regular sound of their oars could still be heard.

Pauline took poor, weeping Madeleine in her arms, kissed and rocked her for a long time and then said: 'Now look. As long as you know it's not your fault. You can't stop men doing stupid things. It was his decision so it's just too bad, that's all.'

Then lifting her to her feet, she added, 'Come on darling! Come and sleep at the house. You can't go back to Le Grillon tonight.' She kissed her again. 'Come on, you'll feel better with us,' she said.

Madeleine got up, still sobbing, but less violently. She leaned her head on Pauline's shoulder. Seeming to find there a safer, warmer refuge and a closer, more intimate affection, she walked slowly away from the scene.

Hautot & Son

The house, half farm and half manor, was one of those combinations often found in the country of a property once vaguely seigneurial and now owned by farmers themselves rich in land. In front of it the dogs tied to the farmyard apple trees were barking and yelping as the keeper and some small boys arrived carrying gamebags.

It was the opening day of the season and in the vast kitchen which served as dining room Hautot senior, Hautot junior, Monsieur Bermont the tax-collector and Monsieur Mondaru the lawyer were having a drink and a bite to eat before setting off on the day's shoot. Hautot senior, very proud of his property, was telling his guests ahead of time what excellent game they would find on his land. He was a big-boned, ruddy-faced Norman, the powerfully built sort of man who can carry a whole barrel of apples on his shoulders. Somewhat authoritarian in manner, he was wealthy, respected and highly influential. He had sent his son César to school up to the fourth form so that he should have some education, then removed him lest he become so much of a gentleman that he no longer cared about his land.

César Hautot was nearly as tall as his father, but leaner. He was an easy-going, happy-go-lucky young man, a good son to his father whom he greatly admired and to whose every wish and opinion he was happy to defer.

Monsieur Bermont, the tax-collector, was a stout little man on whose red cheeks a maze of violet-coloured veins looked like a network of tortuous rivers and tributaries as might be seen on maps in an atlas. He asked, 'And hare? Will there be . . . hare?'

Hautot senior replied, 'As much as you like! Specially round Puysatier.'

'Where shall we start?' enquired the lawyer, a portly, well-fed man trussed up now in a new shooting jacket bought the previous week in Rouen.

'Down at the bottom, I think. We'll get the partridge out on the plain and then put them up from there.'

With this, Hautot senior rose. Following suit they all stood up and stamped their feet to bring warmth and suppleness to the leather of their newly-donned and tight-fitting boots. They collected the guns propped up in various corners of the room, examined the locks, then left the house. Outside, the dogs, still leashed, were now jumping up on their hind legs, yelping shrilly and pawing the air.

They set off towards the lower grounds and a small valley which was no more than a dip of poor-quality land left purposely uncultivated. It was criss-crossed with gullies and covered with fern – an excellent place for game. The guns spread out, with Hautot senior on the far right, Hautot junior on the far left and the two guests in the middle. The keeper and two gamebag carriers followed. Nervously fingering their triggers and with their hearts beating fast they stopped and stood waiting in solemn silence for the first shot of the season to ring out.

There it was! Hautot senior had fired. They saw one

partridge fall away from the headlong flight of birds and come down in a gully covered with thick brush. Highly excited, Hautot leapt up and ran off, tearing up everything in his way and finally disappearing into the undergrowth to pick up his quarry. Almost immediately a second shot rang out.

'The lucky devil!' cried old Bermont. 'He's picked off a hare while he's at it!'

They all waited, eyes fixed on the dense, impenetrable undergrowth. Cupping his hands round his mouth, the lawyer yelled: 'Have you got them?'

Since no answer came from Hautot senior, César, turning to the keeper, said: 'Go and give him a hand, Joseph, will you? We must spread out in line. We'll wait for you.'

Joseph, a great gnarled tree-trunk of a man, set off calmly down towards the gully. Like a fox he carefully reconnoitred the easiest way through the brush. Having found it and disappeared, he cried out suddenly: 'Come quick! Quick! There's been an accident!'

Each man tore through the bushes towards the scene. When they got there they saw Hautot lying on his side, unconscious, clasping his stomach from which long streams of blood were flowing inside his bullet-torn jacket and into the grass. His fallen partridge within reach, Hautot must have dropped the gun to pick it up and in so doing triggered a second shot which shattered his own entrails. They dragged him from the ditch and on removing some of his clothing found a terrible wound now spilling out his intestines. They ligatured him as best they could and carried him home where the doctor they had sent for was waiting, along with a priest.

When the doctor saw him he shook his head gravely, and turning to Hautot's son who was sobbing in a chair, said, 'My poor boy, I'm afraid it doesn't look at all good.'

But when a dressing had been applied, the injured man moved his fingers, opened his mouth, then a pair of haggard eyes, and cast a few anxious glances around him. He seemed to be searching his mind for something and then, when the whole sequence of events came flooding back, murmured: 'Christ almighty! I've had it now.'

The doctor took his hand.

'No! Certainly not! All you need is a few days' rest and you'll be absolutely fine.'

Hautot went on: 'No, I know the score. Shattered stomach. I've had it.'

Then suddenly: 'I want to talk to my son if I've got time.'

Young Hautot whimpered like a little boy: 'Papa! Papa! Oh, poor Papa!'

In a firmer tone his father said: 'Listen, stop crying. Doesn't help. I've got to talk to you. Come close, it'll only take a minute. Then I'll feel much better. You lot, can we have a minute or two if you don't mind?'

The others went out of the room, leaving father and son together. As soon as they were alone the father spoke: 'Listen, my boy, you're twenty-four, I can tell you everything now. Not that there's much to tell. Anyway you know when your mother died seven years ago I was . . . well I'm forty-five now. I was married at nineteen by the way, right?'

'Yes I know.'

'So when she died she left me a widower at thirty-seven.

Can you imagine? Chap like me. Can't be a permanent widower at thirty-seven, can you my boy?'

'No father, of course not.'

The father's face was pale and contorted with pain.

'God, I'm in agony here. Anyway, to continue. A chap can't live entirely on his own yet I couldn't remarry. I'd promised your mum. So . . . are you following?'

'Yes father.'

'So. I took up with this girl in Rouen. Rue de l'Éperlan, number 18, third floor, second door. You are taking all this in I hope? This girl, she's been so good to me, you know. I couldn't have wished for a sweeter little wife. Loving, devoted, you get the picture my boy?'

'Yes father.'

'Well, anyway, if I should pop off I reckon I owe her. A lot. Enough to set her up. You understand?'

'Yes, father.'

'When I say she's a good kid, I mean really good. If it hadn't been for you, and out of respect for your mother's memory, if it hadn't been for this house, and us having lived here, the three of us, I'd have brought her home here and married her, no question. Listen, listen, my boy. I could have made a will but I didn't. Didn't want to. Never put things down in writing. Not that sort of thing anyway. Upsets the family. Makes everything too complicated. Everybody at each other's throats. Who needs legal documents? Don't ever use them. That's how I've made my money, such as it is. Understand, my boy?'

'Yes, father.'

'Listen again, carefully. So I haven't made a will. Didn't

need to. Because I know you. You've got a good heart, you're not ... careful ... tight-fisted, you know what I mean? So I thought when the end came I'd just tell you how things stood and I'd ask you not to forget the girl: Caroline Donet, rue de l'Éperlan, number 18, third floor, second door, don't forget. Listen again. Go straight there when I've gone ... and make sure she's seen all right by me. You'll have plenty. You can do it. I'm leaving you enough. Listen. She won't be there most of the week, she works for Madame Moreau, rue Beauvoisine. But go on Thursday. That's when she expects me. That's my day, has been for six years now. Oh the poor girl! She's going to be so upset! I'm telling you all this because I know you, my boy. Not the sort of thing you tell everybody. Not the lawyer and not the curé. It happens, everybody knows that, but you don't discuss it. Not unless you have to. So, no strangers in on it. Just the family that's all. You understand?'

'Yes father.'

'Promise?'

'Yes father.'

'Swear?'

'Yes, father.'

'I beg of you, my boy, please. Please don't forget. You mustn't.'

'I won't father.'

'Go in person. You're in charge of everything.'

'Yes, father.'

'Then you'll see what she says. I can't talk any more. Swear to me.'

'Yes father.'

'That's good, my boy. Come and give me a kiss goodbye. I'm nearly finished. This is it. Tell them they can come in.'

Moaning, the younger Hautot kissed his father and, obedient as always, opened the door. The priest appeared wearing a white surplice and carrying the holy oils. But the dying man had closed his eyes and refused to open them again. He refused to reply and refused to give any sign that he knew what was going on.

He had talked enough and could not say another word. Besides, he felt relieved now. He could die in peace. What need was there for him to confess to this delegate of God since he had already confessed to his own son who really was family?

The last rites were administered, and he was given communion in the midst of his kneeling friends and servants with never a movement of his face to indicate that he was still alive. He died at around midnight after four hours of spasms indicative of appalling pain.

The season had opened on the Sunday and Hautot was buried the following Tuesday. Having returned from taking his father to the cemetery, César Hautot spent the rest of the day in tears. He hardly slept that night and was so miserable the next day that he wondered how he could carry on living. Nevertheless he spent the whole day thinking that, if his father's last wish was to be carried out, he should go to Rouen the following day and see this Caroline Donet at the rue de l'Éperlan, number 18, third floor, second door. He had repeated this like a mantra so many times so as not to forget it, that now he could think of little else. Both his mind and his ear were hypnotized by the phrase. Accordingly, the next morning around eight o'clock, having ordered Graindorge harnessed to the tilbury, he set off at a brisk pace behind the heavy Norman horse on the main road from Ainville to Rouen. He was wearing his black frock-coat, a tall silk topper and his trousers with the straps under the soles. In the circumstances he decided not to wear over his handsome suit the loose blue smock which, flapping in the wind, protected his better clothes against any dust or spots and which he normally shed as soon as he jumped down on arriving at his destination.

He got to Rouen just as ten o'clock was striking and went as usual to the Hôtel des Bons-Enfants, rue des Trois Mares. There he was embraced by the proprietor, the proprietor's wife and their five sons, all of whom had heard the sad news. After that he had to tell them exactly how the accident had happened and this set him off crying again. He turned down their offers of comfort, all the more insistent now that he was a man of substance, and even refused their invitation to dinner, which really offended them.

Having dusted off his hat, brushed down his frock-coat and given his boots a quick wipe, he set out to find the rue de l'Éperlan. He dared not ask for directions lest he be recognized and suspicions raised. Finally drawing a complete blank, he spotted a priest and counting on the professional discretion of a clergyman found out from him the way to the address. It was very close. In the next street on the right in fact.

He began to feel a little hesitant. Until this moment he had been blindly following his dead father's instructions.

37

Now he felt a confusing mixture of sorrow and shame as he thought of himself, a son, soon to be face to face with the woman who had been his father's mistress. All the old moral strictures lying buried in his unconscious under layer after layer of conventional, received wisdom handed down from generation to generation, everything he had learned from his catechism years and since about loose women and the instinctive mistrust men have of them even if they marry one – all these ignorant, peasant values clamoured inside him, held him back and brought a blush of shame to his cheeks.

Nevertheless, he thought, I promised my father. Mustn't let him down. The door marked 18 was ajar so he pushed it open and saw beyond it a dark stairway which he climbed as far as the third floor. There he saw first one door, then a second with a bell-pull which he now tugged. The tinkle which he heard echo into the room beyond made his heart sink. The door was opened and he found himself standing opposite a very well-dressed, fresh-faced brunette who was staring at him in astonishment.

He had no idea what to say and she, unaware of anything untoward and expecting his father any minute, did not invite him in. They looked at each other for a full thirty seconds, at the end of which she said: 'Can I help you, monsieur?'

He murmured, 'I'm Hautot, the son.'

She started, turned pale and stammered as if she had known him all her life: 'Oh! Monsieur César?'

'Yes.'

'What . . . what's . . . ?'

'I have a message for you from my father.'

She said, 'Oh my God!' and took a step backwards to let him in. He then saw a little boy playing with a cat on the floor in front of a stove where several dishes were cooking.

'Sit down,' she said.

He sat down.

'Well?' she asked.

He was struck dumb, his eyes on the table in the middle of the room laid for three including a child. He looked at the chair with its back to the fire, the plate, the napkin, the glasses, one bottle of red wine, already drunk from, and one unopened bottle of white. That must be his father's usual place with his back to the fire! He was still expected by her! That would have been his father's bread with all the crust removed because of his poor teeth. Raising his eyes, he saw hanging on the wall a large photograph of his father taken at the Paris Exhibition, the duplicate of one which hung over the bed in the master bedroom at Ainville.

The young woman went on: 'So? Monsieur César?'

He looked at her. She was pale with dread and her hands were trembling fearfully as she waited for him to speak. Eventually he gathered up enough courage to do so. 'Well Mam'zelle, I'm afraid Papa died on Sunday on the opening day of the shooting season.'

She was shocked literally rigid. After a few moments' silence she said in a barely audible voice, 'Oh no! He can't have!'

Then suddenly her eyes filled with tears. She raised her hands to cover her face and began to sob. The little boy, seeing his mother burst into tears and deducing that this stranger was the cause, hurled himself on César, grabbed him by the trouser-leg with one hand and started smacking him on the thigh as hard as he could with the other. César, frantic with grief himself, his own eyes still swollen with crying, was moved at the sight of this woman weeping for his father and the little boy defending the mother. He felt almost overwhelmed with emotion and, in order to keep from breaking down himself, started to speak: 'Yes,' he said, 'the tragedy occurred on Sunday morning at eight o'clock . . .'

He went on, assuming she was hearing it all and forgetting no detail, omitting not the smallest incident in a painstaking, plodding peasant way. The little boy continued to smack him and had now begun to kick him on the ankles. When Hautot junior came to the part where Hautot senior had talked about her, the young woman, hearing her own name, uncovered her face and asked: 'I'm sorry. Could you start again please? I wasn't taking it in . . . I really want to know what happened . . .'

He began again, using exactly the same words: 'The tragedy occurred on Sunday morning at eight o'clock . . .'

Again he told her everything, stopping every now and then to punctuate the story with little asides of his own. She listened attentively. With the sensitive perception of a woman, she seized every implication of each twist and turn of events, shuddering with horror and saying 'Oh my God' from time to time. The little boy, seeing his mother had calmed down, stopped hitting César and was now holding her hand, listening too as if he understood every word. When he came to the end Hautot junior said: 'And now what we must do is make sure his wishes are carried out. I'm in a comfortable position. He's left me property so . . . I wouldn't want you to feel in any need . . .'

She broke in abruptly: 'Oh, please, please, Monsieur César! Not today! My heart's breaking! Another time, another day, perhaps. But not today. And if I were to accept, I do want you to know it would not be for me, oh no, no, no, I swear I wouldn't want anything for myself but for the little one. We'll put any money in his name.'

César was aghast. Then the penny dropped. He stammered, 'You mean . . . he's his?'

'Oh yes,' she said.

Hautot junior looked at his half-brother with a mixture of emotions, all deeply painful. After a long silence, for she had begun to weep again, César was at a complete loss as to what to do. He said: 'Well then, Mam'zelle Donet, I'd better be going. When would you like us to meet and talk about arrangements?'

She cried out: 'Oh don't go! Please! Please don't leave me and Émile on our own. I'd die of grief. I've got nobody now except my little boy. Oh it's awful, Monsieur César, it's terrible! Please, please sit down! Talk to me some more. Tell me about what he used to do when he was away from here, when he was back home with you.'

And so César, obedient as always, sat down again. She drew her chair up close to his in front of the stove where the food was still cooking. She put Émile on her lap and asked César hundreds of little intimate questions about his father from which he could see or rather feel instinctively that this poor young woman had loved Hautot with all her heart.

The conversation naturally kept returning to the accident

and he told her all over again what had happened, in the same detail. When he said, 'The hole in his stomach was so big you could have put both hands in it', she gave a sort of cry and began sobbing yet again. This time César too broke down with her and started to weep. Softened by his own tears he leaned down towards Émile whose forehead was within reach and kissed it. His mother struggled to get her breath back.

'Poor little mite,' she said, 'he's fatherless now.'

'Me too,' said César.

At this, each stopped talking. Suddenly the young woman became the practical housewife who thinks of everything and everyone.

'I don't suppose you've eaten a thing all morning, have you, Monsieur César?'

'No, Mam'zelle.'

'Oh, you must be hungry! Will you have something to eat?'

'No thank you,' he said, 'I'm not hungry. Too upset.'

'Oh, but you've got to eat in spite of everything, you'll grant me that. Do stay a bit longer. I don't know what I'll do when you leave.'

After a few attempts at resistance, he sat down opposite her, and in the chair with its back to the fire he settled down to a dish of the tripe that had been sizzling in the oven, and to a glass of red wine. Several times he wiped the mouth of the little boy who had dribbled sauce all over his chin. As he rose to leave, he said: 'When would you like me to come back and talk business, Mam'zelle Donet?'

'If it's all the same to you, Monsieur César, next Thursday.

It'll save me taking time off. I've always got Thursday off anyway.'

'That's fine with me. Next Thursday.'

'You'll have lunch, won't you?'

'Oh, I don't know . . . really.'

'It's much easier to talk over a meal. Saves time too.'

'All right then. Let's say twelve o'clock.'

After giving little Émile another kiss and shaking Mademoiselle Donet's hand he left.

The week passed very slowly for César Hautot. He had never been on his own before and solitude seemed unbearable to him. Until then, he had shadowed his father all his life, following him into the fields, seeing that his orders were carried out, then, after a little while apart, he would see him again at dinner. In the evenings they would sit opposite each other smoking their pipes and talking about horses, cows and sheep. Their morning handshake was an expression of deep family attachment.

And now César was alone. He wandered about in the ploughed fields of autumn, all the time expecting to see the tall silhouette of his father waving to him from some field or other. To kill time he would drop in on neighbours, describe the accident to anyone who had not heard what had happened, and retell the story to those who had. Sometimes when he had run out of things that needed thinking about or doing he would sit down at the side of a cart track and wonder how much longer he could carry on.

He thought often of Mademoiselle Donet. He had liked her very much. He thought she was a very nice person indeed, a good, kind girl as his father had said. Yes, she was a lovely girl. A really lovely girl. He was determined to do her proud and to give her 2,000 francs in interest on capital to be settled on the child. He was rather pleased that he had to go and see her the following Thursday to sort things out with her. The thought of this brother, this new little fellow was a bit of a worry. It bothered him a little, yet at the same time it gave him a warm sort of feeling. There was a bit of kin for him there. The kid born on the other side of the blanket would never be called Hautot, but he was a bit of family with no pressure attached, a bit of his father after all.

When he found himself once more on the way to Rouen on Thursday morning, with these and similar thoughts in his head and the sound of Graindorge's rhythmical clip-clop, his heart was lighter and his mind calmer than at any time since the accident. As he entered Mademoiselle Donet's apartment he saw that everything was laid exactly as it had been the previous Thursday with one single exception – the crust of the bread at his place had not been removed.

He shook hands with the young woman, kissed Émile on both cheeks and sat down feeling both very much at home and extremely emotional. Mademoiselle Donet seemed slightly thinner and slightly paler. She must have cried her little heart out. This time she was a bit awkward in her manner towards him as if she had realized something she had been unable to absorb on that first occasion when she was still taking in the enormity of what had happened. She was extremely attentive to his needs and humble in her approach, as if trying to pay back in devotion and service towards him some of the generosity he was showing her. They took a long time over lunch and discussed the business which had brought him there. She did not want so much money. It was too much, far too much. She earned enough to keep herself; all she wanted was that Émile might have something to look forward to when he reached his majority. César, however, stuck to his guns and even added a present for herself as a token of mourning. As he finished his coffee, she asked, 'Do you smoke?'

'Yes, I've got my pipe here . . .,' he began.

He patted his pockets. Damnation. He had left it at home! He was just about to bemoan the fact when she produced one belonging to his father which she had kept tucked away in a cupboard. He took it from her and recognized it. Sniffing it and with emotion in his voice, declaring it to be one of the best, he filled and lit it. Then he put Émile on his knee and played ride-a-cock-horse with him while she cleared the table, stacking the dirty dishes in the sideboard to wash later after he had gone.

At about three, when he rose regretfully, he hated the idea of leaving.

'Well, Mamz'elle Donet,' he said, 'I'll wish you a very good afternoon. I'm delighted to have made your acquaintance like this.'

She remained standing in front of him, blushing and near to tears. As she looked at him she thought of his father.

'Are we not to see each other again then?' she asked.

He replied simply: 'We can, Mam'zelle, if that's what you'd like.'

'It most certainly is, Monsieur César. Shall we say next Thursday, if that's convenient for you?'

45

'Indeed it is, Mam'zelle Donet.'

'You'll come for lunch, of course?'

'Well, if you're offering I wouldn't say no.'

'Very well, Monsieur César. Thursday next it is, at twelve o'clock, like today.'

'Twelve o'clock on Thursday then, Mam'zelle Donet!'

Laid to Rest

Five friends had been dining together. They were all rich, middle-aged men of the world, two of them bachelors, three married men. These monthly meetings of theirs were some of the happiest evenings of their lives. They had all known each other since their youth, remained close friends, enjoyed one another's company and often stayed talking till two o'clock in the morning. The conversation was about anything and everything that might interest or amuse a Parisian and, as in most drawing rooms, it was a kind of verbal version of the news in the morning papers.

One of the most footloose and fancy-free among them was Joseph de Bardon, a bachelor who exploited to the full all the attractions Paris has to offer. Though not exactly decadent or debauched in his habits, he managed to satisfy all the natural curiosity of a fun-loving man in his late thirties. A man of the world in the best and widest sense of the word, he was witty rather than profound, knowledgeable rather than wise and possessed a quick rather than a deep understanding of human nature. His experiences and encounters provided him with a fund of anecdotes, some edifying, some frankly hilarious. He had a reputation in society as a bright fellow with a good sense of humour – everyone's favourite after-dinner speaker whose tales were always the ones most looked forward to. He never needed any urging to begin, as he did on this occasion.

47

Certain creatures at certain times and places look absolutely in their element, let's say a goldfish in its bowl, a nun in church, or what have you. Sitting there smoking a cigar, with his elbows on the table, a half-filled glass of liqueur brandy to hand and relaxing in a warm haze of coffee and tobacco, he looked like a man in his ideal milieu. Between a couple of puffs he spoke.

'The funniest thing happened to me not so long ago . . .'

A near-instantaneous chorus replied, 'Go on, do!'

And he was off.

'Thank you, I shall. You know I get around Paris a fair amount. As other people window-shop, I watch what's going on. I watch the world and his brother pass by, I watch what's going on around me. Well, some time towards the middle of last September, I left the house one afternoon with no clear idea of where I was going. You know how you always have a vague yen to go and see some pretty woman or other . . . you riffle through your little black book, you do a few mental comparisons, you weigh up the possible delights and you decide more or less on the spur of the moment. But when the sun's shining and it's warm outside you don't always want to be cooped up indoors. On this particular day, it was warm and sunny and I lit a cigar before starting to stroll along the outer boulevard. As I was sauntering along I decided to make for the cemetery in Montmartre and have a little wander about there. I like cemeteries, you know. They sadden and they soothe me and I find I need that from time to time. And of course some of one's chums are there, people nobody goes to see any more. I drop by every so often still.

And as it happens, an old flame of mine is buried in Montmatre Cemetery, a lovely little lady I was very keen on at one point in my life, very attached to. So although it's painful, I find it does me good. I mean all kinds of memories come flooding back while I'm there, letting my thoughts drift beside her grave. It's all over for her of course . . .

'The other reason I like cemeteries is because they're like cities in themselves, densely populated at that. Just think how many generations of Parisians are packed in there for ever; so many people stuck in their caves, their little holes just covered with a stone or marked with a cross, while the living take up so much room and make such a stupid racket.

'Then of course you've got all the monuments, some of them much more interesting than in a museum. Though I wouldn't put them in the same league, Cavaignac's grave reminded me so much of that masterpiece by Jean Goujon, the statue of Louis de Brézé in the underground chapel at Rouen cathedral. That's actually the root of all so-called modern, realist art, you know. That statue of the dead Louis de Brézé is more convincing, more terrible and more suggestive of inanimate flesh still convulsed in the death-agony than any of the tortured corpses you see sculpted these days on people's tombs.

'But in Montmartre Cemetery you can still admire the impressive monument to Baudin, the one to Gautier, and that to Murger, on which incidentally, only the other day I spotted one poor solitary wreath of helichrysums. I wonder who put that there. Perhaps the last of the *grisettes*, now a very old woman and possibly one of the local concierges. It's a pretty little statue by Millet, suffering badly from neglect and all the accumulated dirt of the years. Oh for the joys of youth, eh, Murger?

'Anyway there I was, stepping into Montmartre Cemetery, suddenly filled with sadness of a not entirely disagreeable kind, the sort that makes a healthy fellow think "Not the most cheerful of spots, but thank God I'm not stuck in here just yet." The feeling of autumn, the warm dampness of dead leaves in pale, weak sunshine heightened and romanticized the sense of solitude and finality surrounding this place of the dead.

'I wandered slowly along the streets of graves where neighbours no longer call, no longer sleep together and never hear the news. Then I started reading the epitaphs. I tell you gentlemen, they are absolutely killing. Not even Labiche or Meilhac can give me more of a laugh than the language of the headstone. When you read what the nearest and dearest have put on the marble slabs and crosses, pouring out their grief and their best wishes for the happiness of the departed in the next world, and their hopes – the liars! – for a speedy reunion, it's hilarious! Better than a Paul de Kock any day!

'But what I love most in that cemetery is the deserted, lonely part planted with all those tall yews and cypresses, the old district where those who died long ago now lie. Soon it will become the new part of town; the green trees nourished by human corpses will be felled to make room for the recently departed to be lined up in turn under their own little marble slabs.

'After I had wandered about long enough to refresh my mind, I realized I was now getting a little bored and that it was time to go to the last resting place of my old love and pay her my ever-faithful respects. By the time I reached her graveside I was feeling quite upset. Poor darling, she was so sweet, so loving, so fair and rosy . . . and now . . . if this spot were ever opened up . . . Leaning on the iron railings I whispered to her a few sad words which I dare say she is unlikely to have heard. I was just about to leave when I saw a woman in deep mourning on her knees at the next graveside. She had lifted her crêpe veil and under it could be seen a pretty head of fair hair, a crown of bright dawn under the dark night of her head-dress. I lingered. In what was obviously deep distress she had buried her face in her hands and, stiff as a statue, was deep in meditation. Absorbed by her grief and telling the painful beads of memory behind closed and hidden eyes, she seemed herself dead to the world in her loss. Suddenly I saw that she was about to break down. I could tell from the slight movement her back made, like a willow stirring in the wind. She wept gently at first then more and more violently with her neck and shoulders shaking hard and rapidly. All of a sudden she uncovered her eyes. Full of tears they were lovely. She looked wildly about her as if waking from a nightmare. She saw me looking at her, seemed ashamed and buried her whole face once more in her hands. Then she burst into convulsive sobs and her head bent slowly down towards the marble slab. She rested her forehead on it and her veil, spreading about her, covered the white corners of her beloved sepulchre like a new mourning-cloth. I heard her moan before she collapsed with her cheek against the tombstone and lay there motionless and unconscious.

'I rushed over to her, slapped her hands and breathed on her eyelids while reading the simple epitaph beyond:

HERE LIES LOUIS-THEODORE CARREL
Captain of Marines
Killed by the enemy at Tonkin

PRAY FOR HIS SOUL

The date of death was some months earlier. I was moved to tears and redoubled my efforts to revive her. Finally they succeeded and she came to. I'm not bad-looking, not yet forty, remember, and at that moment I must have been looking extremely solicitous. At any rate, from her first glance I realized she would be both polite and grateful to me. I was not disappointed. Between further tears and sobs she told me about the officer who had been killed at Tonkin after they had been married for just one year. He had married her for love. She had been an orphan and possessed nothing but the smallest dowry.

'I comforted her, consoled her, lifted her up, then helped her to her feet.

"You can't stay here like this," I said, "come on . . ."

"I'm not sure I can manage to walk . . ."

"I'll help you, don't worry."

"Thank you, Monsieur, you're very kind. Did you have someone here yourself you wanted to mourn?"

"Yes, Madame."

"A lady?"

"Yes, Madame."

"Your wife?"

"A . . . friend."

"One can love a friend as much as a wife. Passion has its own laws."

"Indeed so, Madame."

'We walked away together, she leaning on me so heavily that I was almost carrying her along the paths of the cemetery. As we were leaving it, she said: "I think I'm going to faint."

"Would you like to go in and sit down somewhere? Let me get you something to . . ."

"Yes thank you, I would."

'I noticed a place nearby, one of those restaurants where the friends of the recently buried go when they have completed their grim duties. We went in and I made her drink a cup of hot tea which seemed to restore her strength somewhat. A faint smile came to her lips and she began to tell me a little about herself. How sad, how very sad it was to be all alone in the world, to be alone at home day and night, to have no one with whom to share love, trust and intimacy.

'It all seemed sincere and so genuine the way she told it. I felt my heart softening. She was very young, twenty at most. I flattered her a little and she responded gracefully. Then, as time was getting on, I offered to take her home by cab. She accepted. In the cab we were so close to each other, shoulder to shoulder, that we could feel the warmth of each other's bodies through our clothing – one of the most disturbing feelings in the world, as you know. When the cab drew up in front of her house she murmured: "I really don't think I can get up the stairs on my own. I live on the fourth floor. You've been so kind . . . could you possibly give me your arm again, please?"

'I said of course I could, and she went up slowly, breathing hard all the time. Then at her door she added: "Do come in for a few moments so that I can thank you."

'In I went, naturally.

'It was a modest, not to say poor little apartment furnished in simple but good taste. We sat side by side on a little sofa where she started talking again about how lonely she was. She rang for her maid to bring me something to drink. No one appeared. I was delighted about this and imagined that this maid must work mornings only, in other words, she only had a cleaner. She had taken off her hat. She really was quite a charmer. Her lovely, limpid eyes were fixed on me with such a clear, direct gaze that I suddenly felt an irresistible urge. I succumbed on the spot and clasped her in my arms. On her eyelids, which had instantly closed, I rained kiss after kiss after kiss. She struggled, pushing me away and repeating: "Please . . . please . . . please . . . have done!"

'What exactly did she mean? In the circumstances there were two ways of interpreting the words. To silence her I moved down from the eyes to the mouth and, putting my preferred interpretation on her request to please have done, complied with it. She put up little resistance and when later we looked at each other again after an insult to the memory of the captain killed at Tonkin she wore a languorous expression of tender resignation which dispelled any misgivings of my own.

'I showed my gratitude by being gallant and attentive, and after an hour or so's conversation asked: "Where do you normally dine?"

"At a little restaurant nearby."

"All on your own?"

"Yes, of course."

"Will you have dinner with me tonight?"

"Where did you have in mind?"

"Oh, a very good restaurant on the boulevard."

'She demurred for a while but I insisted and finally she gave in, reasoning that she would otherwise be terribly lonely again. Then she added, "I'd better change into something less severe," and disappeared into her bedroom. When she emerged she was in half-mourning and wearing a very simple but elegant grey dress in which she looked slender and charming. She obviously had markedly different outfits for the cemetery and for town.

'Dinner was very pleasant. She drank champagne, became very animated and excited, after which I went back to her apartment with her. This little liaison begun between the tombstones went on for some three weeks or so. But novelty, particularly with regard to women, eventually palls. I dropped her on the pretext of some unavoidable trip I had to make. I was very generous when we parted and she in turn very grateful. She made me promise, no, swear, to come back on my return and really seemed to care a little for me.

'I lost no time in forming other attachments, however, and about a month went by without my having felt any particular desire to resume my funereal fling. But nor did I forget her. The memory of her haunted me like some unsolved mystery, a psychological teaser, one of those nagging little puzzles you can't leave alone. One day, for some inexplicable reason, I wondered whether, if I went back to Montmartre Cemetery again, I might bump into her, and decided to return.

'I walked around for a long time but there was no one there apart from the usual sort of people who visit the place, mourners who have not yet severed all ties with their dead.

At the grave of the captain killed at Tonkin no one mourned over the marble slab, no flowers lay there, no wreaths. However, as I was walking through another district of the city of the departed I suddenly saw a couple, a man and a woman in deep mourning, coming towards me down a narrow avenue lined with crosses. To my amazement as they approached, I recognized the woman. It was she! Seeing me she blushed. As I brushed past her she gave me a tiny signal, the merest glance, but conveying in the clearest possible way both: "Don't show you know me," and "Come back and see me, darling."

'The man with her was about fifty, distinguished-looking and well-dressed, with the rosette of the *Légion d'honneur* in his lapel. He was supporting her just as I had done when we both left the cemetery that day.

'I went off, flabbergasted by what I had just seen and trying to imagine what tribe of creatures she belonged to, hunting as she obviously did on this sepulchral terrain. Was she a single prostitute who had struck on the brilliant idea of frequenting graveyards and picking up unhappy men still haunted by the loss of a wife or a mistress and troubled by the memory of past caresses? Was she unique? Or were there more like her? Was it a professional speciality to work the cemetery like the street? The loved ones of those laid to rest! Or was she alone in having conceived the psychologically sound idea of exploiting the feelings of amorous nostalgia awakened in these mournful venues?

'I was longing to know whose widow she had chosen to be that day.'